Lena Semaan has been a
journalist and author for over twenty-five years.
She has worked for Penguin and ghost-written
several books for Random House, working with
public figures including Jacqueline Gold, John Bird
and Noel Edmonds.

About Diffusion books

Diffusion publishes books for adults who are emerging readers. There are two series:

Books in the Diamond series are ideally suited to those who are relatively new to reading or who have not practised their reading skills for some time (approximately Entry Level 2 to 3 in adult literacy levels).

Books in the Star series are for those who are ready for the next step. These books will help to build confidence and inspire readers to tackle longer books (approximately Entry Level 3 to Level 1 in adult literacy levels).

Other books available in the Star series are:

Not Such a Bargain by Toby Forward

Barcelona Away by Tom Palmer

Forty-six Quid and a Bag of Dirty Washing by Andy Croft

Bare Freedom by Andy Croft

ONE SHOT

LENA SEMAAN

First published in Great Britain in 2016

Diffusion
an imprint of
SPCK
36 Causton Street
London SW1P 4ST
www.spck.org.uk

ISBN 978-1-908713-04-9

Typeset by Graphicraft Limited, Hong Kong
First printed in Great Britain by Ashford Colour Press
Subsequently digitally reprinted in Great Britain

Produced on paper from sustainable forests

Contents

1

Boxing

They were shouting for him now.

'Come on, mate. You've got him.'

'Hit him. You can do it.'

Dan was bobbing and weaving as the punches came at him fast.

'Good one, Dan.'

'Careful, he's testing you now. Don't fall for it.'

The punches kept coming.

The shouts grew louder. The crowd were urging him on; they were all behind him.

'You can do it, Dan. Come on, boy. You can do it.'

He ducked as the punch slid by his face, ducked again, once more and then he heard the bell. It was over.

*

People often call boxing just fighting, which proves they have no idea what it is all about. You need skill, speed, grace and discipline. You cannot just get into the ring, put gloves on and box.

You have to put in a lot of work that has nothing to do with wearing boxing gloves or punching a bag. Or punching an opponent. You need a lot of skill. It also pays to have a chin like rock.

First there is the running. Running gives boxers their fitness and there is no getting away from it. Dan ran six times a week, at least five kilometres a day. He often ran much further. The distance was important but he had to do speed drills as well. He did them up a steep hill. Standing at the bottom, eyeing up the hill, he told himself to work through the pain. That is the only way. You can always be fitter and stronger. There are no limits once you start.

Every session in the gym starts with skipping. Skipping helps you become fast and quick and it makes you light on your feet. Plus it gets you warmed up very, very fast.

Dan had hated skipping when he started. He watched the guys around him, who made it look all so easy with their fancy jumps and criss-cross ropes. He was amazed at how light on their feet some of the bigger, heavier guys were. Some weighed as much as a hundred kilogrammes but they landed on the ground, just as light and dainty as a ballet dancer. He watched as they hopped sweetly from foot to foot, whipping the rope round, hardly moving their wrists.

After skipping, it is time for the technical drills. Shadow boxing, travelling, bobbing and weaving. Technique can always be fine-tuned. This applies to learning the punches as well. It is not enough to punch hard. You have to be able to save your punches for when they matter. Your feet have to be in exactly the right place if you want to throw a knockout punch. And if you are unsteady on your feet, your hands will be everywhere and your punches weak.

Boxing depends on everything working together. Legs. Arms. Brain. If you do not have the legs for it, you get tired pretty quickly. Then your hands start to drop. No matter how good you are, if you get tired, you are in trouble. Your opponent will see it and know he has a chance of knocking you down. He will wait for your hands to lower, then send in a whole lot of quick-fire jabs. Then you are in trouble.

Clean punches are what you are after and they are all built on the jab and the cross. The jab is true to its name: a fast, stinging pop of a punch. It blocks the other guy's view of your opposite hand. Then you come in with the cross. This is more of a power punch. The power comes from rotating your body. The one-two combo, they call it.

The usual boxing position for right-handers is left foot in front of right. The idea is that your weaker side is the one closer to your opponent, leaving your right hand to come in with the power punch.

Dan was left-handed and was known as a 'southpaw', which meant he put his right foot in front of his left. A good southpaw fighter is a tricky opponent.

In the past few years Dan had changed his diet from his usual junk food and fried breakfasts to a diet where he watched everything he ate. Well, mostly. He ate clean, which meant chicken or fish plus vegetables. These days he hardly ever drank. Sometimes, after a night out, he would pig out on a Maccy D's (or three) but he always got back on track the next day.

He was proud of his body and there was good reason for that. He looked fit and he looked good. He especially liked his shoulders: they were not too big, but defined. His arms were strong and lean. And of course he had the boxer's flat, tight, six-pack. He was proud of himself, proud of the fact he had got there by working hard.

'You'll be showing off those abs on the cover of *Men's Health* soon,' his mates said. Dan liked hearing that. There were worse things people could say to you, for sure.

*

Now he stretched back against the ropes, getting his breath back. He had done it. Gone the distance with Snowy, one of the best amateur boxers around, a bloke with ten times more experience than him.

Dan was dripping with sweat. He looked at his opponent. Snowy got his name because he had platinum white hair. Just now he also had a thin film of shiny sweat on his face and his hair was shimmering in the light. Snowy was sweating but he was not puffing hard like Dan, even though he was fifteen years older.

'Good one, Dan.' Snowy wrapped him up in a bear hug. 'Some good combos in there.'

'Thanks, mate,' replied Dan. 'That means a lot coming from you.'

It felt good. Not just to hear he had done well from someone he respected. It always felt good to be at the boxing club, with this group of people. This was his family. These people, they understood him and cared about him. They looked out for him and he did the same for them.

There was another thing he liked about boxing. There are rules: a code of doing things, and everyone has to stick to it. Anyone who does not follow the code is not going to stay long. There is no room for making up your own rules. Not in a place like this.

Sometimes Dan thought about how the world would be better if people could live their whole life like that. If they just did what they were supposed to. He remembered when he was at school and they learned about laws. 'Laws are there to protect everyone,' said the teacher.

That sentence had stuck in his head. He liked the idea that laws protected you. But he knew they did not really do that. Some people did not care about laws. They did not care about hurting someone else. And they got away with it.

What do you think?

How is boxing different from fighting? Why does Dan enjoy it so much?

'Laws are there to protect everyone.' In what ways is this true or false?

If you could choose just one rule for your own life, what would it be?

2

Family

As Dan came out of the changing room, Neil Robson, the boxing coach, came up to him.

'Come and have dinner with me and Rosie,' said Mr Robson. 'She hasn't seen you for a while. She's been asking about you. I know she's making your favourite meal tonight.'

Neil Robson was more than just the coach at the club. He was the boss. He was the one who made the rules. He was an ex-professional who had been on the coaching teams of some of the biggest names in boxing. Now in his late sixties, he was still lean, strong and as fit as a flea. He followed the same tough training schedule he had been following since he was eighteen. People respected Mr Robson. They listened when he started speaking. They listened because he knew what he was talking about. Plus he was a really good guy.

When Dan first turned up at the club, he was a skinny, nervous, twelve-year-old.

Mr Robson took him under his wing and treated him like a son. That was almost seven years ago. Dan had never met anyone like Mr Robson and his wife Rosie before. They were like a real family, how he had imagined a family would be.

He liked going to their house. It was cosy and felt safe and secure. Most of all, it was calm. Nobody yelled in this house. Well, except when the grandkids came over, ran around and went crazy. Dan loved it when they were there. He was an only child and he had always wanted brothers and sisters. It was a new experience to be in a house where people came and went, talking and laughing. The walls of the house were full of family photos. Everywhere you looked there were memories of good times spent together.

And there was Molly, their dog. She was a brown, woolly, bouncy dog who just wanted to play all the time. When Dan came to visit, Molly would greet him, her chewed-up teddy in her mouth. Dan would throw the toy in the air and Molly would catch it with her mouth. Or sometimes she would play it cool and just ignore it. He liked to lie down on the floor with her and rub her warm tummy as she rolled around. Then Molly would make a low growling sound that said she was happy, and the world was OK.

There was always a warm hug from Rosie and a proper meal at the table. It might not be flash like those plates of food you see on *MasterChef*. The food was not fancy but it was cooked well and homemade.

Dan liked the way they made dinner into an occasion. Even if it was just pasta, the table was set and everyone sat down to eat together. It didn't matter who was there – they all sat around talking and having fun. It was like the sort of thing you saw in those American TV series where everyone always sat together to eat. Dan wondered if he was the only person who noticed that everyone on American TV was always eating. They did it in the movies too. Dan had once read that Brad Pitt eats something in every movie he's in. Someone said it was because it showed off his jawline. Someone else said it was because he'd given up smoking. Whatever it was, he always had food with him.

'You know you're always welcome. You don't have to be invited,' Mr Robson had told him in the past. 'You're one of the family now.'

Neil and Rosie Robson had been good to him. Sometimes he could not believe how kind they were.

After all, who was he? Just another kid from a messed-up family.

Dan would have liked to accept the invitation to dinner tonight, but he knew that he could not.

'Nah, Mr Robson,' he said. 'Mum isn't feeling so hot. I'd better go home and see what she needs.'

Dan always called him 'Mr' when he spoke to him. It felt right to address him that way. He could not call him Neil. That would not be proper.

Mr Robson replied, 'Well, give her my best. And take that worried look off your face. The world isn't going to cave in. Not just now, anyway. You did well today.'

'Yes, Mr Robson,' said Dan. 'See you tomorrow.'

*

When Dan got home that night, he heard the noise of TV laughter. His mum was watching an old American programme, one of those sitcoms where two families lived across the road from each other and interfered in each other's lives. Nothing much happened really, mostly talking, except they managed to make it funny.

It was really old, like from the 1970s or something.

He could understand why his mum liked programmes like this. It was just a bit of fun that you could get lost in for a while and you would feel better afterwards. Mum always said that that was what TV was for: to give you a break. Those old programmes, they were sort of innocent. There were problems, but not like the ones on *EastEnders* where everyone was miserable. On these old shows, nothing was ever going to ruin your life. Plus, whatever the problem was, it would always be solved by dinnertime, when everyone would be happy again.

His mum spent a lot of time watching TV. Some days she did not get dressed. She did not like to go out much. She thought people were looking at her and that made her feel insecure.

Most of the time she was in pain because of the broken bones in her left hand. They were not broken now but they had never healed up properly. Her fingers were curled up almost the whole way, all the time.

She looked pale, he thought. Spending a lot of time indoors did not help but she really did not look OK. He knew that some days were very bad. She took a lot of painkillers and then felt sick.

That was because they were so strong, but she needed them.

'Hi, Mum.' Dan hugged her. 'How are you feeling?'

'I had one of my turns,' she replied. 'It came on all of a sudden and I felt dizzy.'

'Mum, you need to see the doctor when that happens. I've told you that,' said Dan.

'I'm fine,' said Mum quickly. 'Don't worry, it happens all the time.'

'That doesn't mean you should ignore it, Mum,' he said. 'It's telling you something.'

'It's telling me I'm an old lady?' she joked.

She was forty-one. These days that was young. Women looked fit and healthy in their forties. But not his mum. She looked like she had been in too many boxing rings.

She tried to change the subject, like she always did.

'How was your day?' she asked.

'I held my own against Snowy,' he said with a grin.

'Well now, that's something. He's very good, isn't he?' said Mum with a smile on her face.

'He's better than good,' said Dan. 'I don't know how he keeps doing it. He barely broke a sweat.'

'I'm sure he was sweating underneath,' laughed Mum.

'Nah, no way,' said Dan, shaking his head. 'Snowy is a machine.'

Dan saw the open box of painkillers on the table next to her. They were the extra-strong ones. He did not like her taking them, though he knew she needed to.

'Mum, you haven't been taking too many of those things, have you?' he asked. 'It's not good for you.'

He knew that she drank a bit of wine with them too. Not a lot. 'It's my extra medicine,' she used to say.

'Stop worrying,' she told him. 'I take what I need. Don't think about that. It's late. You need to eat and get some rest. You have to get up for work early. Now stop fussing. I'll be all right.'

'But Mum,' said Dan, 'someone has to worry about you, so it had better be me.'

'I'm so lucky to have you,' said Mum, giving him a hug.

She wasn't lucky. Far from it.

What do you think?

Lots of families do not sit down to eat together these days. Why does this matter? Or doesn't it?

Why do you think Dan calls Neil Robson 'Mr Robson' and not 'Neil'?

Why does Dan worry so much about his mum? Who do you worry about the most?

3

Broken

Dan made himself a protein drink and came back into the lounge. He looked at his mum, sitting in her chair like an old lady. She never felt anything but pain. His father had seen to that.

The constant beatings his dad had given her had left her bruised and battered. Destroyed. Dan had seen his dad hit her in the nose, smack her round her face, pin her up against a wall and try to strangle her. Sometimes his mum would try to push him away and then his dad would go in harder, calling her names. Dan begged his dad to stop but his dad never listened.

His mum would tell Dan, 'Shut up, or you'll make it worse.'

She kept taking the punches. She took them like Muhammad Ali took them from George Foreman. He'd watched their famous fight, the 'Rumble in the Jungle'. At the start of the second round, Ali leaned on the ropes and covered up.

All defensive, he let Foreman punch him on the arms and body. Foreman threw loads of punches and used up his energy. When he got tired Ali came in and got him with some sharp jabs. 'Rope-a-dope', Ali had called it.

But Mum was not George Foreman. And Dad was not Muhammad Ali. A man like Ali had principles. He would never hit a woman. His dad was a common thug.

One day, when Dan was ten, he got in between them. 'Please don't hurt my mum. Please, please stop,' he'd screamed. Mum had begged him to get out of the way. She told him to go to his room and stay there. His dad had lifted his hand to him, as if he was going to hit him. Dan remembered waiting for the blow but it never came. Instead, his dad picked him up, took him up to his room and locked the door.

Dan never understood why his dad did not beat him too. Mum told him never to interfere again. 'This isn't about you, Dan. It's between us.'

Dan was angry, not just with his dad but with her. How could she say it wasn't about him? How could she say something so stupid?

Even after his dad had beaten her to a pulp, and given her bruises on top of bruises, his mum would defend him.

'He cares about me, Dan,' she used to say. 'He just doesn't know how to show it. He has trouble keeping his anger under control. He's not being himself.'

She even told Dan that his dad hit her because it was her fault.

'I don't do what I'm supposed to,' she said. 'It makes him angry and he can't help himself. It's just his way. He just wants me to do the right things.'

'Mum,' Dan said, 'he's an animal. He hurts you for no reason. It's wrong.'

But she kept finding excuses for him. And it got worse.

'Your dad is not well,' she would say. 'He is sick and he doesn't know what he's doing. He's really a good man. He doesn't mean it and you know he loves you.'

Bollocks. He wasn't sick. He was a violent, cruel man who deserved to be locked up. Or killed.

When he was younger, Dan had never understood why nobody came and stopped it all.

The neighbours must have known what was happening. The houses on their new estate were jammed in together tightly and the walls were as thin as paper. The neighbours must have heard his dad yelling. And they must have heard his mum screaming when she could not take the punches any more, then crying, long into the night. He had cried too.

As he got older he learned how it works. People are scared. They do not like to get involved in violence. It is worse if it is domestic violence. Nobody wants to stick their nose in where they are not wanted. So they pretend they have not seen or heard anything. And even though they did hear it and they saw the bruises and cuts on Mum, nobody said anything. Everyone pretends it is OK. Or they just don't look.

Where were the police? They did not seem to be interested. Families were complicated. And Mum never complained to them. She did not want the police to visit. She was scared that his dad would hit her again. Or worse still, he might leave. Mum was terrified of being left, but Dan reckoned it would be the best thing to happen to them.

Some people seemed to guess something was not right, though. The teachers noticed that he was not paying attention. He stopped eating. When he was ten he stopped going to school for a while, but then they told his parents. He thought his dad would beat him up, but he did not. Instead, he started driving Dan to school and making sure he went in. His dad would pretend to be interested in his schoolwork and stuff. As he drove he would talk to him like a normal dad, asking questions about school. He kissed him as he got out of the car. 'Have a good day, son.' It was like living with Jekyll and Hyde.

Now, Dan looked at his mum's hands resting in her lap. Her 'alien' hands, she called them. He remembered the day it had happened. He could see it like it was today.

Seven years ago, his dad had come home drunk, shouting. His dad forced his mum to put her hands in the doorway, and slammed the door. Dan remembered the blood, and the sound of her hands breaking. It was a sound that made him want to vomit. His mum was screaming. Dan remembered screaming too.

And then his mum went quiet. Like she was in shock or something. Her face was white. Dan didn't care if his dad hit him; he was going to call an ambulance.

They came in ten minutes. Dan felt like his whole life was rushing past him. It was like being in a dream. So he did not notice that his dad was no longer there. At some point between Dan calling the ambulance and it arriving, he must have slipped out.

Dan was sure that his dad would come back. But after they took his mum to hospital the cops sent a policewoman to get Dan and take him to Auntie Em's house. The policewoman talked to him and asked him about his dad.

She was from a special unit that helped families like Dan's. He thought she was really nice. But he found it hard to talk. He'd been so used to keeping things to himself. She asked a lot of questions.

'Did he ever beat you?'

'Did he threaten to beat you?'

'How long has this been going on? Can you tell us?'

Dan could not remember. He just said, 'For ever.'

The cops did look for his dad but they could not find him. His mobile number was not working. Dan figured he must have tossed the phone in a rubbish dump somewhere. They asked around, but if his dad's mates had seen him, they were not letting on. Bastards, thought Dan. They're protecting him.

The policewoman finished asking him questions. Dan was seriously tired now. He just wanted to close his eyes and sleep. Someone wrapped a blanket round him. He heard a voice say, 'We'll be back to check on you.' It might have been the policewoman but he was not sure. He slept for almost two days.

His mum was in hospital for a long time. And then she came to stay at Auntie Em's. This time she did not tell the cops to mind their own business when they asked questions. But she was still stubborn.

They asked her if she wanted to move to a women's refuge.

'No,' she said. 'I'm going back to my house.'

Auntie Em pleaded with her not to. 'He'll be back. They always come back. Stay here for a while at least.'

'No, this time he's gone,' his mum said.

She looked sad, which surprised Dan. All he could think of was that they would finally be free of the hell they had been through. That was all he wanted.

What do you think?

Why does Dan's mum defend his dad when he beats her up? Is she right to say it's her own fault? If so, why?

Dan's neighbours knew what was happening but never got involved. If you were one of his neighbours, what would you have done?

Do you think a child ever forgets seeing what Dan saw? How might it affect the rest of a child's life?

4

Good things

About six months after his dad left, Dan saw
the advert for the boxing club. That was the
day things began to change.

At first he thought it was some programme for
goody-goody kids, run by someone who could
not box but had this stupid idea they could teach
other people how to. There were lots of people
like that about.

Dan did not know anything about boxing.
All he knew was that he had not been able to
protect his mother and he never wanted to feel
like that again. So he went to the club. After
the first day he realized it was not run by some
two-bit nobody. Mr Robson was the real deal.
He began to look forward to it. For the first time,
he felt doors were opening in his life, instead of
slamming in his face.

He learned to box. He discovered he was
good at it. Mr Robson also welcomed him into
his family and showed him what family life could
be like.

It was through the club that he found work when he left school. He had not really thought about work when he was young. He could never imagine life going anywhere, not the way things were. He figured that it was better not to hope, because then he would not be disappointed. Other kids dreamed their dreams. He just got on with trying to survive.

At the club there was a bloke who knew somebody, who knew somebody else. That was how it worked. He got the job. And not just any job: he was a plumber's apprentice. One more year to go now and he would be fully qualified.

The money was good and it would get even better. People always joked with him about getting rich. 'You will never run out of work,' they told him. 'You will be busier than a gravedigger and as expensive as a lawyer!' They were right about being busy. He had been snowed under lately. He was amazed at how dumb people were. They just poured anything down their drains. Where did they think it went? People could be so stupid.

He worked with Tom Arnott, who was a funny old character. The side of the van said 'Arnott and Sons'. The fact was, there were no sons. It was just a name. Tom told him that people liked family businesses. They liked to think they were putting their drains in the hands of someone who really cared about what they did. That made Tom laugh.

Dan liked his work. There was always something new. Today they were working on a new café in the high street. Its name sounded Italian. Casa Di Mia or something like that. The owners had promised them a free meal when the work was done.

'I don't like foreign food,' said Tom.

'It's not foreign,' said Dan. 'It's stuff you've had before like spaghetti and pizza but, you know, sort of posh.'

'Posh pizza! Dough with tomato and cheese? What's posh about that?' joked Tom.

Tom made Dan laugh with the things he said sometimes. Although he was never sure if Tom was joking or not.

Dan liked eating out. Maybe if the café was good, he would take Casey there one day. Casey was his girlfriend. He had met her three months ago when she came to pick up her fourteen-year-old brother, Joe, from a boxing class.

Dan had been helping Mr Robson take the class. The boys and girls were all aged from eight to fifteen years. Dan loved teaching the kids. He took them through the warm-up drill and then through some pad work. Joe was a good kid.

When Casey walked in, Dan clocked her straight away. Funny how you can do that even though you almost have your back to someone. Dan had felt his knees go wonky.

Casey's smile did not just light up her face. It lit up the whole room. She had a fresh-looking face, and long brown hair, dark eyes and long lashes. She was the kind of girl who looked really comfortable with herself. You could tell by her walk. It was confident and she had a spring in her step. She wore a pair of ripped jeans, Converse and a sweatshirt. Dan thought she was the prettiest girl he'd ever seen. And everyone in the whole place noticed it.

'Oooh, look at Dan. He's gone all wobbly,' said one of his mates.

'He's gone all funny and shy,' said another mate.

'Dan, keep your mind on the job,' Mr Robson said with a smile on his face.

Casey saw it all and she threw him a look. After Joe had collected his things and they were leaving, she turned back to look at him. He blushed red like a beetroot. The guys ribbed him for days after that. All he could think about was if she would come again at the same time next week. He hoped so. But not too much. You don't want to hope too much.

She turned up the next week. When he saw her, something inside him felt like going 'Yippee', but he was doing his best to play it cool. Stupid idea, he thought. Why did you have to pretend you didn't like someone when you really liked them? Whoever made that up was an idiot.

Casey strolled in. She had a way about her, partly because of her confident walk and how she looked everyone straight in the eye. They shared another look. What was he supposed to do? He'd been in nightclubs and found it easy to talk to girls, but that was when it did not really matter. They were just girls you talk to for the fun of it.

Don't go yet, Casey, he thought to himself. He turned round to put some equipment away. When he turned back, she was right by him. He was speechless.

'Did I scare you?' she asked.

'Um . . . uh no. No way,' he stuttered.

'Good,' she said. 'Well, here's my number. See you Friday.'

And that was all she said before she walked out with Joe.

Dan was stunned into silence.

'Well, she's got you sorted,' said Snowy.

Dan had the biggest grin on his face. He was smiling so much his face hurt. They could take the mickey out of him but it would not stop him smiling.

Dan and Casey went out the following Friday. The plan was to see a film, but Casey said that maybe they should save that for next time.

Wow, she already wanted a 'next time'!

'Let's just go somewhere and talk,' she suggested.

'Do you like spicy food?' he asked. 'Not Indian, but Mexican stuff. You know, tacos?'

Casey smiled. 'I love it!' she said.

They had two kinds of tacos, beef and chicken, plus some dips.

Around them people were doing tequila shots but Casey was not interested and Dan was not bothered either. She asked for dessert, though. He liked that. Most girls just wanted to share what was on your plate and that really pissed him off. They had a Mexican chocolate pudding.

'It's so light and creamy, it's like eating chocolate clouds,' said Casey.

They spent the night chatting about anything and everything. He felt so relaxed with her. He could not believe how easy it was, much easier than with any other girl he had met. He did not feel like he had to think about every single thing he said in case he sounded like an idiot. She made him feel good.

It was one of those nights when you were having such a good time, you don't even watch the clock. He was glad. Before they met up he had been really nervous that they would end up like those couples who spend the whole night saying nothing to each other. All they do is look at their mobiles.

They were still there, deep in conversation, when the staff started putting up chairs on the tables around them.

'Something tells me it's time to go,' said Dan.

On the way out, he held Casey's hand.

'You're so easy to talk to,' he told her.

'Why, do you find it hard talking to other women? I never got that impression from you. Ooh, look, you've gone red again,' she teased.

'It's not that. It's just . . . well . . . there are things you can't tell everyone,' said Dan shyly.

'What kind of things?' said Casey. 'You can tell me.'

'Oh, you know. Stupid stuff,' said Dan. 'Anyway, it's late. I'd better make sure you get home.'

He didn't answer the question. She didn't push it.

A few weeks later, though, she asked him again. 'What is it, Dan? Come on, if we're going to be mates you have to tell me stuff.'

'I tell you everything,' he said. 'More than I've ever told another girl.'

'That's not the point,' insisted Casey. 'You're all bottled up. Sometimes I worry that you're going to explode!' He smiled. She kissed him.

'I will tell you,' he promised. 'When I'm ready.'

What do you think?

Why does Tom Arnott put 'Arnott and Sons' on his van even though he does not have any sons? Do you think it is a good idea or a bad idea? Why?

How has joining the boxing club made a difference to Dan's life?

Casey says to Dan, 'You're all bottled up. Sometimes I worry that you're going to explode.' Do you ever feel like this? What is the best way to cope if you do?

5

Unfinished business

Mr Robson knew about Dan's dad. They had not
discussed it much but Mr Robson seemed to be
aware of what had happened to him. These things
get around. A few years ago, when Dan was
sixteen, Mr Robson had asked him if he felt angry.

'Well, yeah, I do sometimes,' Dan told him. 'And
sometimes . . . I just wish I could kill him and then
I would know he can never hurt Mum again.'

'You know you can't do that,' said Mr Robson,
shaking his head. 'But you can focus on what
you've got now and try to make a good life,
where violence isn't the answer.'

Yeah, easy for you to say, thought Dan.

People always said that the past was over
and done with. They said that you could not do
anything about it. It was best to put it behind
you, they said, because no good could come
of bringing it all up again. Dan understood
that. But he reckoned that there were
some things that were never behind you.

And a violent childhood, well, it wasn't easy to forget. Even if you tried, it stayed with you.

Every day he was reminded of what had happened. Not just the sad figure of his mum, but all the stuff in his head. He found it hard to trust people and to form close relationships. For a bloke who could punch his way out of almost anything, he was like a rabbit in the headlights sometimes. Childhood cannot be something that is just in the past. It's the place you go to when you want to feel safe and loved, even as an adult. And if you cannot do that, you're stuffed.

He did his best to get on with his life. 'Look at the good things you have,' Mr Robson was always telling him. It was all coming together now. His job. Casey. But every day he felt hurt by his past. He always had a sense of unfinished business.

Lately it had been playing on his mind more than usual. Some nights he would lie awake and imagine how he could have killed his dad. He wished he could have ended all his mum's troubles. He had a few ideas about how he might get rid of him.

There was a TV programme, a documentary, about a woman who killed her husband. It was one of those shows where they reconstruct a true story. She had really put some thought into it because she decided to grind up glass and put it in his food. It looked just like sugar. Her husband ate it and then his insides began to bleed. He died soon after he got to hospital. The trouble was, she got caught. The trail was too obvious. Even the dumbest PC Plod would figure that one out.

He liked the idea, though. It seemed a bit smarter than sneaking up behind him with a hammer and hitting him on the head. Although that would be pretty quick. Bam. All done. It seemed so easy when you thought about it like that, but of course it wasn't.

He had read about some kids in America who killed their violent father. But that was different. Their father had just murdered their mother in front of them. The thought terrified him. The idea that in one split-second, you could make a decision that would change everything.

He had spent a lot of time wondering how people killed someone and got away with it. Mind you, they never really got away with it for long. Especially if it was someone they were related to. Everyone knew that the cops started by interviewing the family. That was how it worked.

But what if you could make it look like an accident? Plenty of people have accidents.

He used to imagine following his dad to the station when he was on his way to work. It would be early in the morning, when his dad wouldn't expect it. He would get to the platform and then Dan would sneak up and push him in front of a speeding train. He could say that his dad jumped a bit too far forward because he was surprised to see him.

Better still, he imagined the phone ringing and his mum answering it. The news was bad. His dad had been crushed to death in a broken lift on the building site. Or he had been electrocuted. Or he had fallen under a truck. It never happened.

There had been times when his dad would go all quiet. Sometimes, Dan would come back home from school and his dad was there but not talking. That was tricky. Like living with a time bomb. His dad could be a real charmer. Lots of people used to say what a good guy he was.

But, Dan knew it would just be a matter of time before his dad turned into an animal. It was amazing how he hid it from the rest of the world. How he saved his anger and his fists for the moment he stepped inside the front door. If he did that, thought Dan, he must know what he was doing. He wasn't really out of control. Otherwise he would have fights with everyone.

People told Dan he should just get on with his life now that his father was gone. But Dan still felt as though his dad was there with them in the house. His Auntie Em had wanted them to move house so that they could make a fresh start. But Mum would not hear of it. She wanted to stay where she was. Dan did not blame her. She did not have the strength in her to move. On some days when she woke up she looked like she had gone ten rounds with Snowy. Most of the time she looked like a crumpled piece of paper.

What do you think?

Mr Robson says that 'violence isn't the answer'. Is physical violence ever right? Why or why not?

Dan thinks that if you grow up in a home where you don't feel safe and loved 'you're stuffed'. What makes him think this? In what ways is he right or wrong?

'In one split-second, you could make a decision that would change everything.' Have you ever made a split-second decision that's changed everything? Would you make the same decision again? What might you do differently?

6

Mission

Dan was a man on a mission. He had a practice session at the club for the 'City Boys v. Tradies' boxing night.

This was a big show that Mr Robson helped to organize every year. The night was a programme of fights where flash city boys were matched against those in a 'trade', which meant basically anyone who wasn't a flash city boy. White collar versus blue collar. The City Boys sponsored the event and each year it got bigger and bigger. They always put on a wicked party afterwards. The entrance fee went to a charity that organized programmes for kids across London.

Mr Robson was in charge of coaching the boxers and getting them into shape. To be in it, they had to sign up three months before the show and commit to every training session. Women did it too. Even beginners were taken on and taught. If Mr Robson decided they could handle being in the ring for three two-minute rounds, he would match them up with people

who were at the same level. When they were
all in their boxing shorts, gloves and protective
headgear, they were all equals, all in it
together.

Dan had done the show for three years. At first
it surprised him how seriously everyone took the
training. Most of them were not regular boxers.
Many had never even tried it. However, the
evening was organized professionally. There was
always an ambulance on hand, a doctor at the
ringside and proper health and safety. So far
nobody had got hurt, except for the odd bruise
and a lot of bloody noses.

Even though the boxing was taken seriously,
the night itself was fun and everyone got into
the spirit of the thing. They even had 'boxer'
nicknames. Some of the city boys really took
the mickey out of themselves. There was an
investment banker who called himself Dan 'Midlife
Crisis' Stevens and an accountant known as John
'Mr Boring' Wilson.

As well as a nickname, each boxer got to
choose his or her own theme tune. 'Eye of the
Tiger' was a popular one. Everybody wanted it, so
they had to do a draw for it. So was LL Cool J's
'Mama Said Knock You Out' and DJ Shaled's
'All I Do Is Win'. He liked AC/DC's 'Thunderstruck'.

That was Manny Pacquiao's song. But Dan made his entrance to Eminem's theme from *8 Mile*, 'One Shot'.

Dan had become friendly with a few of the city boys and he liked them. He often sparred with them, usually a guy who called himself Ash 'Almost Amir' Khan. Ash was from a Pakistani family, born and raised in Leicester. Ash played the flash boy but he wasn't really the boastful sort. He was smart, though – a successful foreign exchange trader who worked for a big bank in Canary Wharf.

In a world full of white boys, Ash was a rare thing. He was often the target of comments from colleagues. Some of the comments were just banter. Other comments were nasty. Ash gave it right back to them. The City was full of international workers and mostly they just fitted in, but being from a Pakistani family was not seen as international, more like something to look down at. It didn't matter that Ash was more successful than most of them.

Dan had a lot of time for Ash. He was one of the funniest, coolest guys around. Who cared what colour he was?

When they had first met, Dan had no idea what Ash did all day. It sounded pretty good, though.

'So let me understand this. You trade money?' Dan asked.

'Well, yeah,' Ash said. 'You play one currency off against another. For example, the Japanese yen against the Australian dollar. You bet on how they're going to move. Up or down. Dead easy.'

It sounded simple, but Dan reckoned that if it was that easy, everyone would be doing it.

Whatever he did, Ash seemed to have a lot of fun doing it. He and some of his city trader mates seemed to spend a lot of their time at work just messing around. They were always egging each other on to do stupid challenges. Like the time they decided to see who could lose the most weight in a week. Ash had told Dan about it. He spent so long in the sauna that week that he almost passed out. One of the others took laxatives. They weighed themselves daily. Ash was positive he had it in the bag until the weigh-in, when some German trader called Roland beat him. 'The guy did bloody nothing all week and then we have a weigh-in Friday and he's lost eight freakin' pounds. Still don't know how he did it. They beat us at everything, Germans. Clever bastards.'

Ash was already waiting for him when he arrived. Dan enjoyed their practice sessions.

It wasn't just the boxing, he enjoyed the banter too. They were not fighting each other in the show, but they were both fast so they always sparred well together.

'Wotcha, mate,' said Ash.

'Hey, Ash. How's things?'

'Sweet, mate. Sweet.'

Things were always sweet with Ash. He had a good nature. He had recently bought his parents a new house. And he liked a bit of bling. When he was not boxing, one wrist was weighed down with a huge Rolex, with diamonds set into its face.

'Wow,' said Dan, feeling his eyes widening until it was impossible for him to open them any further.

Ash shrugged. 'Oh, this little baby? You should see my other one.'

They climbed into the ring and a trainer helped them on with their helmets. Amateur boxers always had to wear headgear. It made sense. Those punches were harder than they looked.

'You gotta go easy on me. I'm just a boy who sits on his arse all day,' joked Ash.

'Too late,' said Dan as he whipped some quick jabs in.

It was a good session. In the changing room, Dan asked, 'Got time for a quick word, Ash?'

'Sure, mate,' said Ash. 'What's up?'

'I need your help to find someone,' said Dan. 'I don't think it will be too hard, but I don't want anyone here to know. Can you do it?'

Dan knew that if Mr Robson found out he was looking for his dad, he'd stop him.

'You in something messy?' asked Ash. He looked a bit worried.

'Nah, nothing like that,' said Dan. 'I just want to find my dad. I haven't seen him for years and I think it's time we got together. Anyway, you know a lot of people and I wondered if you could get an address for me. I mean, if you can't, that's cool, mate. Don't want to put you to any trouble.'

He saw a look cross Ash's face. Maybe he should not have asked him. Ash was a very smart guy. He would work out that something might be up. Dan knew Ash didn't believe his story. But if Ash was thinking anything, he didn't say it. He just said, 'I've got a mate. He's a private investigator. I'll sort it and nobody will know it happened. In fact it didn't happen, OK.'

Ash did what he promised. Next day, Dan got a text from him. It was an address. Mission accomplished.

Dan was surprised. The address was not far away. It would probably take an hour or so to get there. The idea that the man who had hurt his mother was so close made him feel desperately sick.

Underneath the address Ash had simply put, 'Use it wisely, mate.'

What do you think?

Ash laughs off the rude comments about his family being from Pakistan. What are the best ways to deal with being insulted?

What would your boxing name and theme tune be?

Ash gave the address to Dan even though he suspected something was up? Why do you think he did this? What do you think Dan will do now that he knows where his dad is?

7

Secrets

Dan needed to clear his head. Now he knew
where his dad lived, and he had to figure out
what to do. The fact was, he had no plan. Not
a bloody clue. As he looked at the text from Ash,
he thought of what his dad had done to his mum
and felt sick to his gut. He had to make that
feeling disappear.

The next day, he could not keep his mind on
his work. He was fidgety. He dropped things.

'Butterfingers,' said Tom. 'You get enough sleep
last night?'

Dan sighed. 'Sure, I'm just a bit clumsy today.'

Later, when he saw Casey, he felt uncomfortable.
It was worse with her, because she felt every shift
in his moods. He had never known anyone like
that. He could not hide stuff from her. She was
far too smart not to see it, much smarter than
he was. What was it they called it? Women's
intuition.

She was on to him from the start.

'Something's wrong, isn't it, babe?' asked Casey. 'I feel like you're in another country. What's going on in that head of yours?'

'Nothing, Casey. Really,' he said. 'Nothing for you to worry about.'

'Ah, that's where you're wrong,' said Casey. 'Because I do worry. I worry because I care. And I care because I love you, Dan. I really do.'

He was stunned. It was like she'd knocked him out with a one-two.

That was the first time she had said it. The 'L' word. He looked at her.

'I mean it. I love you, Dan,' she said again. 'I really think we have something here. I hope you do too. And I don't want anything to come between us and mess this up, OK? Promise?'

Dan smiled. 'Promise,' he said.

He reached for her and pulled her into him, holding her tight. He wanted to wrap her up in cotton wool and never let go of her. The prettiest, kindest girl in the world had told him she loved him. He had never heard anyone say those words to him before. Never.

She pulled her face back from his and looked at him. He had tears in his eyes.

Casey stroked his face. She tried again. 'Come on, tell me what's wrong, babe.'

'Nothing. Nothing,' he answered. 'It's just that this is so good and I don't deserve it.'

'You do, Dan. You deserve lots of good things. Now stop it or you'll make me cry.'

Dan said, 'I love you, Casey.'

'I love you too, Dan.'

Dan had never told anyone the details of his life, especially not a girlfriend. Now he found himself opening up to Casey, telling her about his dad's reign of terror in the house and what had happened to his mum.

She didn't react or say much. Instead she just held his hand tightly and listened.

'I just wanted to disappear, you know?' he told her.

'Disappear? Like how?' asked Casey.

'Dead. I just wanted to be dead,' replied Dan.

For a moment he was worried that he had put her off.

'Sorry, I didn't mean to tell you all that stuff, Casey.'

She stopped still and took his face in her hands. 'Dan, I'm not just here for the fun bits.

I love you and I care about you, so stop saying sorry.'

They say that when somebody loves you, you see things differently. Dan felt like he had been struck by lightning. In a good way.

They were in the park, and he looked around him at the parents playing with their kids. He had never imagined that one day he could be one of them. Until now the thought of building a life with someone else and making his own family had not occurred to him.

Here, with Casey, a lot of things seemed possible. A young dad, not much older than him, was kicking a plastic football with his toddler. The father was laughing as the kid picked up the ball and came running all the way to give it back to him. 'You're not allowed to handball,' he said. 'Red card.'

Dan watched him scoop up the chubby little boy and give him a big squeeze and a kiss. The way he held him, it was like he wanted to keep him safe.

Had his own dad ever held him like that? Had he ever wanted to protect him? Dan realized that he could not remember anything about his dad when he was little. It was as if his memory had been wiped out. And he did not want to ask his mum about it.

After his dad left, Dan and his mum never spoke of him. There were times when he felt that if only he knew the whole story about his dad, he could close the book and have that future everyone kept talking about. Right now, even living in the present was troubling him. He knew he could not leave the past behind unless he did something. Something dramatic.

'I'm going to have an early night,' he said to Casey.

'Come home with me?' she asked.

'I'd love to, but sometimes a man has to make sacrifices. I need to get up really early,' said Dan.

'Sure?' She looked at him from underneath her long dark eyelashes.

'Yes. Just tonight. I'll come and bother you tomorrow.'

*

When he got home there was nobody there. He thought that was strange because his mum only went out when his Auntie Em took her. But today it was Thursday and Auntie Em never normally came on Thursdays because she was off doing good deeds for charity. She liked being helpful.

The TV was still on so he went upstairs to check if his mum had just got tired and gone to bed. She was not there. Her handbag was there, with her glasses. She would not go anywhere without them. She was as blind as a bat. Something must have happened to her. His heart began to race and beat fast. What if . . . what if . . . his dad had come and done something to her? He felt himself grow warm, then hot. He broke into a sweat.

Just then his phone rang. It was Auntie Em.

'Your mum's had a bit of a bad turn. She's in hospital,' said Auntie Em.

'Why didn't you call me?' Dan asked.

'I did, but your phone was off,' explained Auntie Em.

He raced to the hospital and found his mum. She was lying in a bed, hooked up to a drip and with lots of tubes in her. She looked as white as a sheet and there was a cut on her head. Her nose was bruised.

'Mum, what happened? Did Dad hurt you?' asked Dan.

'Don't excite her now,' said the nurse. 'She fainted. We think it's a problem with her low blood pressure but we're not sure. We're doing some tests.'

'I don't believe you,' he said. 'He hit her again, didn't he? He was there!'

'No, that's not it, I can assure you,' the nurse said patiently.

'He came, didn't he?' said Dan. 'Tell me the truth, Mum, and I'll stop it ever happening again. I promise.'

'No, Dan.' She could hardly speak. 'Nobody came. I just fell. Don't worry. They'll fix me up.'

That was the truth. But it didn't matter. He was angry that his mum was in hospital. It was all his dad's fault. This had only happened because he had beaten her up all the time.

Dan looked at her lying in the hospital bed. She didn't look like his mother. She looked like his grandmother. She had lost the best years of her life.

He suddenly felt rage surge through him. 'Mum, I'll be back tonight. And I'll look after you. I promise.'

He stormed out of the double doors of the hospital and got into his car. He tapped the address Ash had given him into the sat nav. This should not take long. What he was about to do was long overdue. He should have done it a long time ago.

What do you think?

Casey tells Dan she loves him. Why do you think that makes him emotional?

Why hasn't Dan ever thought about having a family before?

Why is Dan so angry that his mum is in hospital? Is he angry with his mum, his dad or himself?

8

Choices

If you kill someone who is violent, do you get rid of the violence? A long time ago, Mr Robson had asked him that question. It was when he first joined the club.

He had seen Dan punching the bags in frustration. 'You're hitting, but you're not hitting effectively because you're too angry,' he told him.

'So what?' Dan demanded.

'So, being angry is not going to help you,' Mr Robson explained. 'Boxing is also about control. It's about the brain, the feet and the hands all coming together. And after it's done, you leave it in the ring.'

'But what if you have to defend yourself?' Dan asked.

Dan knew that Mr Robson had taught the odd bloke a lesson. There was the time he was in the pub with Rosie and some punk grabbed her bag and ran off with it. Mr Robson sprinted after him and soon caught up with him.

Apparently he pinned the thief to the footpath. The thief struggled to get free, but Mr Robson held him firmly on the ground.

He had not hurt the thief. But he told him that if he fought back he would flatten him, good and proper. The guy kept trying to escape, but still Mr Robson just held him tight.

'Why didn't you hit him?' asked Dan.

'What's the point?' shrugged Mr Robson. 'He was a nobody, just a two-bit thief. I had him. He was bloody annoying, he kept wriggling and mouthing off. But he was not worth my time.'

Mr Robson used the thief's own mobile to call the police. Then he held on to him until they came.

Mr Robson said to Dan, 'With power comes responsibility. When you have the ability to hurt somebody, you have to think very carefully. If it's a matter of life and death and self-defence, then you have a reason. But if it's just some prat, you need to be able to sort out the problem and get rid of it without using force.'

*

Dan sat in his car on the way to his dad's. 'Nobody really understands the crap I've gone through,' he said to himself. 'Not even Mr Robson.'

Today he had a chance to fix it once and for all. Then he could finally put it behind him, just as everyone wanted him to do. Then he would be free. This was how he would get justice. It was payback for all those years his mum had suffered. Otherwise it would never end for her, or for him.

His mobile rang. He saw it was Casey so he pulled over to answer it.

'Where are you?' she said.

'I've just been to see Mum in hospital,' he explained. 'She's had a turn. She's very weak. Her blood pressure is really low and they're doing tests.'

'Oh, Dan, do you want me to come?' she asked.

'No, babe. Really, it's OK. She's in good hands. I've just got to go and finish a bit of work now. I'll catch you later, OK?'

'Dan, you sound strange,' said Casey.

'Nah, you're just imagining things. Honestly, I'm fine,' insisted Dan.

'If it's something to do with your mum, it's not fine,' Casey said sharply. 'Don't lie to me now, Dan.'

He was feeling edgy and he did not want a conversation about this now. He did not want Casey involved in any of this.

It was the first time he had raised his voice to her.

'How many times do I have to tell you?' he shouted. 'It's fine. You're reading too much into this. Sometimes you're too clever for your own good, Casey.'

He could tell she was upset. She went quiet. Casey wasn't a girl who sulked. But he'd make it up to her later, when the mess was all cleaned up.

He hung up on her.

He was headed west, out past Heathrow somewhere. His dad had not gone far. He had not needed to. If he had beaten up someone other than his wife, he would be in jail by now. But domestic violence was complicated, they said. You had to be careful. And his mum had not pressed charges, so his dad was technically free. Even the court injunction might not be worth the paper it was written on. So Dan had good reason to make sure it would not happen again.

What do you think?

Why does Dan lie to Casey? How does he feel about it?

What do you think Mr Robson means when he says, 'With power comes responsibility'?

If Dan hurts or even kills his dad, will he be free? Why?

9

Dad

Dan parked his car a few streets away from his dad's address, and then got out and walked the rest of the way. The street where his dad lived was full of flats, ugly blocks that were built in the 1970s and had never been looked after. There was rubbish everywhere: food, clothes and some parts from a bike. The rest of the bike had probably been stolen.

The house Dan and his mum lived in wasn't a palace, but it was better than this. Even he felt uncomfortable in this neighbourhood, and that was saying something.

Flat number 38A was up some stairs. The stairwell stank of urine. It was rank. His boxer's training meant he stepped lightly and quietly as he walked down the ugly, concrete hallway. He did not want to make too much noise.

He arrived at the flat. It had a grey, metal door that looked like it belonged in a prison. There was a window that looked out on the common space.

God knows why anyone would want to look outside, though. It was depressing.

The grubby curtains at the window hung slightly open. He looked in. It was the kitchen. It was pretty basic. He could see a small table against the opposite wall. It had a mug, a plate and a saucepan on it. There was a cooker next to it. He could see newspapers piled up on the floor.

He stepped back and listened. He thought he heard the sound of a radio but he could not be sure it was coming from this flat.

Dan did not know exactly what he had expected to find but he was surprised. He wasn't even sure what he was doing here. He just felt that he had to do something. It was long overdue.

There was a message on his phone from Casey. She wanted to talk. Now. He thought about how happy he felt being with her. After this he would go back home and he would patch things up with her. What he was doing here was fixing the past. If he made that right, then he and Casey could have a good future without him always looking backwards.

Out of the corner of his eye, he saw movement inside the flat. It was him. His father.

For some reason he had imagined him to be a strong, fit man. This person was not what he had imagined. He was thin, and his face was red and full of veins. He looked much older than he was supposed to. He was dressed in tracksuit bottoms, slippers and a T-shirt that looked like it never came off.

Any doubts Dan had about who this man was disappeared when he saw the wedding ring. It was unusual, a silver band with a black stone, and he wore it on his middle finger. He'd never taken it off.

Dan watched him put the kettle on and spoon coffee into the mug. He looked slow and tired.

It doesn't matter what he is now, he thought. He's still a wife-beater and he deserves to pay for what he's done.

'Justice. That's what this is about,' said Dan to himself. If he did not do it then his dad would go unpunished. The thought that he actually had a father made Dan feel sad. Over the past few years he had tried not to think about it. He told himself he never had a dad. It seemed to hurt less if you thought like that.

Something else bothered him. He could not remember celebrating his birthday at all.

He looked at his phone. Casey would be well pissed off if she found out what he was going to do now. Why would anyone care? He was not going to kill his dad. He just wanted to teach him a lesson, one that he would never forget. 'I shouldn't be standing here thinking about it,' he told himself.

But something was holding him back.

Was it the thought that Casey would find out? He was no good at hiding stuff from her. Even trying to surprise her with an outing never worked. His face gave everything away. She once said to him that he would be a terrible spy. True. Casey was already on to him. That was why he had shouted at her in the car.

He didn't want to lose Casey. She was special. If she walked away from him, that would be it. Casey was not the type of girl who came back to you. She did not need to.

He knew that he was putting their relationship on the line. There was a lot at stake here. He was getting all confused now. It should have been easy to come here and do what he had to. After all, nobody cared about the old bloke in 38A, did they? If anything happened to him, who would give a damn?

But it didn't feel like it did when he'd got in the car to come here. Instead he felt a huge wave of sadness wash over him. It was not something he was used to. Usually if he thought about his dad he felt rage, but right now, watching him live his little life, he pitied the bloke.

He walked back towards the stairwell and went down the stairs, past a rat sniffing through a pile of rubbish. If it wasn't a rat then it was a mouse on steroids. He stood on the stairs trying not to breathe in the stink around him.

He was thinking about what Mr Robson might say. Though he treated Dan like a son, he was a man who applied his rules to everyone. He would have to kick Dan out of the club. A few years back, a guy was told to leave after abusing a nightclub bouncer. The guy had been outside the nightclub and sounded off about how he could take anyone on. He got abusive when the bouncer stopped him going into the nightclub and then he got aggressive. When word got back to Mr Robson, he didn't mess around. He did not want that kind in the club. 'You cross one line and you don't stop crossing them,' he said.

There was someone coming down the steps. His dad. Except he wasn't his dad any more.

He was just this man. Dan stepped back into
the shadows so he could watch without being
seen. His dad shuffled out into the middle of the
common space. It was meant to be a garden but
really it was just a big slab of concrete with some
weeds growing through.

Dan watched him take out a cigarette, and
light up. That was all he had. A few walks
outside now and again to smoke a cigarette.
He had thrown his life away when he threw
his punches.

Maybe that was his punishment? He deserved
to be punished for what he had done. At the
same time, it was just like Mr Robson said. Family
was the biggest line of all. This bloke, who
seemed to be a complete stranger to him, was
his father. As much as Dan hated him, he knew
that even though his dad had crossed a line, he
could not do the same thing. It had to end here.

He watched his dad walk back up to his flat,
back to nothing. For a moment Dan thought
about saying something, but there was no point.
This man had cut himself out of his family and
out of life. He had no more choices.

On the other hand, Dan could choose. There
was no good that could come out of this, only
bad. It had to be left here.

What do you think?

Why do you think Dan feels sad when he sees his dad again?

Mr Robson says, 'You cross one line and you don't stop crossing them.' Have you ever 'crossed a line' in your life? If so, when and why do you think you did it?

How would you describe the difference between justice and revenge?

10

New beginnings

There was music pumping out of loudspeakers at the old fruit market near the City. This was where the 'City Boys v. Tradies' charity event would be held in a few hours. Tonight, Dan would be the headline act. He would swagger down the walkway, through onlookers and well-wishers on either side of the barrier and into the ring. Right now he stood in his normal clothes, taking in all the preparations.

The event was always black tie. The guests paid good money for their tickets. Over the years this had become the main white-collar boxing event in the City. Big businesses, like law firms and banks, would book several tables each. A table with ringside seats cost about five grand. Standing-room-only tickets were twenty quid each. All the tickets were sold out months ago and some had changed hands more than once. Charity boxing events were popular.

After the fights there would be an auction where the punters would bid silly money for holidays, handbags and watches. All the goods were donated by businesses willing to support a good cause in return for positive publicity. City types loved to be seen spending money and did not care if they paid five times what an item was actually worth. What they cared about was that they won the bid and that the crowd saw them do it.

At first, Dan had been really surprised by the people from the City. He had expected them to be quiet, serious and boring. But that was not the case. When the fights started they were loud, especially the women, and they enjoyed a good laugh.

Dan watched the waiting staff as they went round the tables making sure everything was in place. There were flowers in the centre of each table, white tablecloths and gleaming silver cutlery.

The DJ was here too, doing a soundcheck and making sure he had the entrance songs in the right order. A boxer would not want to walk to the ring with someone else's song playing. If the DJ got it wrong, Dan was sure there would be a riot.

Dan heard a voice behind him.

'Hello, Dan. Feeling good?'

It was Mr Robson. Dan was happy to see him.

'Sure am,' he said. 'Bit nervous, though.'

'Listen to me,' said Mr Robson. 'Just forget you're the headline act and do what you do best – fight. You'll be fine. Keep your eye on him, though. Don't get cocky.'

'Don't worry. I won't,' said Dan.

'How's your mum?' Mr Robson asked. 'I hear she's much better now.'

'Yeah,' Dan said. 'They really checked her out at the hospital and looked after her. She's even eating better now too.'

'That's good to hear. Is she coming tonight?' asked Mr Robson.

'No. But Casey will be here.'

Mr Robson smiled and said, 'You're keen on her, aren't you?'

'Well, yeah, I am. We . . . uh . . . get on well.'

'She's a great lass. You're lucky to have her,' said Mr Robson.

'I know,' agreed Dan.

Mr Robson looked thoughtful. 'I'm really proud of you, Dan. You've got your life together when I know it hasn't been easy for you. This is the beginning of good things for you and I hope you realize that.'

For a moment Dan was a bit worried. Did Mr Robson know about the visit to his dad? If he did, he had not said anything about it.

Neither had Casey. When he came back he told her what he had nearly done to his dad. 'I'm so sorry for yelling at you, Casey. It was out of order. I'm so disgusted with myself for doing that.'

Ash waved at him from across the room, his diamond ear studs glinting in the light. He came over and put an arm around Dan.

'You planning to blind your opponent with those rocks?' Dan asked.

'Nah.' Ash smiled. 'These are my little ones. How are you anyway, mate? Did you sort out that business?'

'Yeah,' said Dan. 'I took your advice.'

Ash did not say anything for a moment. Then he looked pleased.

'Good man. That's how we roll.' Ash gave him a warm hug. 'Later, mate.'

'Later,' said Dan.

He headed for the dressing room to warm up. This was the best part. He loved it. He could hear the announcer introducing his fight.

He heard the crowd chanting. Eminem was blaring through the speakers. Dan paced the small dressing room until he heard his name called out.

The noise of the crowd became a loud roar, followed by whoops and cheers. Dan walked out into the light. One shot, he told himself. Make it count.

What do you think?

It has ended well for Dan but it could easily have ended differently. What might have happened if Dan had beaten his dad up? Should he have tried to make up with his dad? Is he better off without him?

Do you think Dan's relationship with Casey changed him? If so, how?

Events in our past can affect our future. Should we let go of them? What else could we do?